DATE DUE

CARLETON PLACE
PUBLIC LIBRARY

Trouble Talk

by Trudy Ludwig

Illustrated by Mikela Prevost

Foreword by Charisse L. Nixon, Ph.D.

Tricycle Press
Berkeley/Toronto

FOREWORD

We all have a universal need for connection and a sense of belonging. However, it is important to realize that we can meet this need in constructive or destructive ways. *Trouble Talk* is a story about a girl named Bailey who tried to get those needs met in destructive ways. Sadly, Bailey is not the exception. In our culture we learn to connect with others by sharing negative information (*"Did you hear about _______?"*) or information that isn't necessarily ours to share (*"Guess what I heard?"*) or by offering unsolicited opinions or advice (*"No offense but . . ."*). Researchers have found that females are particularly vulnerable to falling into this "trouble talk" trap. This makes sense given that girls are socialized in this culture to develop close relationships with others by sharing secrets . . . sometimes their own and sometimes other peoples'. One of our jobs as adults is to teach boys and girls how to develop healthy, intimate relationships *without* sharing information that is not theirs to share.

Sharing others' troubles establishes bonds and is exciting and powerful. But it can also be a double-edged sword that cuts down children. The need for power and status among peers can lead to spreading rumors, building alliances, exclusion, and a myriad of other destructive behaviors symptomatic of relational aggression. Unfortunately, the

fallout from trouble talk includes broken relationships and feelings of betrayal that can last well into adulthood. It would be far better for children to learn early on how to develop and maintain friendships using constructive, healthier talk in which they help, rather than hurt, each other and share their hopes, dreams, and goals.

Trouble Talk is a story about what can happen when a child passes on someone else's information as a way to establish connection, feel powerful, and gain attention. Trudy Ludwig does a beautiful job of describing what "trouble talk" is, and the harmful consequences it carries, in a way that children can understand. Like other books by Trudy, her *solution-based* focus provides young readers with real strategies to deal with everyday friendship issues. *Trouble Talk* is a must-read for any child who is trying to understand how to fit in, whom to trust, and how to make friends.

Charisse L. Nixon, Ph.D.
Penn State Erie, The Behrend College
Director of Research for The Ophelia Project®
Co-author of *Girl Wars: 12 Strategies That Will End Female Bullying*

I know a girl who has a really big mouth. Her name is Bailey. Big Mouth Bailey. She doesn't know I've called her that because I've never said it out loud. But that's what I think.

When Bailey came to Hoover Elementary, my teacher, Mrs. Rodriguez, picked me to be her Welcome Buddy.

I was shy around her at first. I was afraid I'd say something stupid and she wouldn't like me. But Bailey started chatting away, asking lots of questions about our school and the kids who go here. It felt good to tell her what she wanted to know.

We sat together every day at lunch and talked about all kinds of stuff. Bailey never ran out of things to say. And she told the funniest jokes.

Everything was going great—until Keisha's sleepover.

"Let's play *Truth or Dare*," said Bailey. "I'll go first. Keisha—truth or dare?"

"Truth," she giggled.

"No offense, but that shirt you're wearing is way too small. Did your clothes shrink or are you just getting fatter?"

Keisha's mouth dropped open.

"That wasn't very nice," I said.

"Oh c'mon, it's just a game," said Bailey. "Besides, I'm doing her a favor by telling her the truth."

"Some favor," mumbled Keisha.

"Girls," called Keisha's mom. "Come and get your ice cream sundaes!"

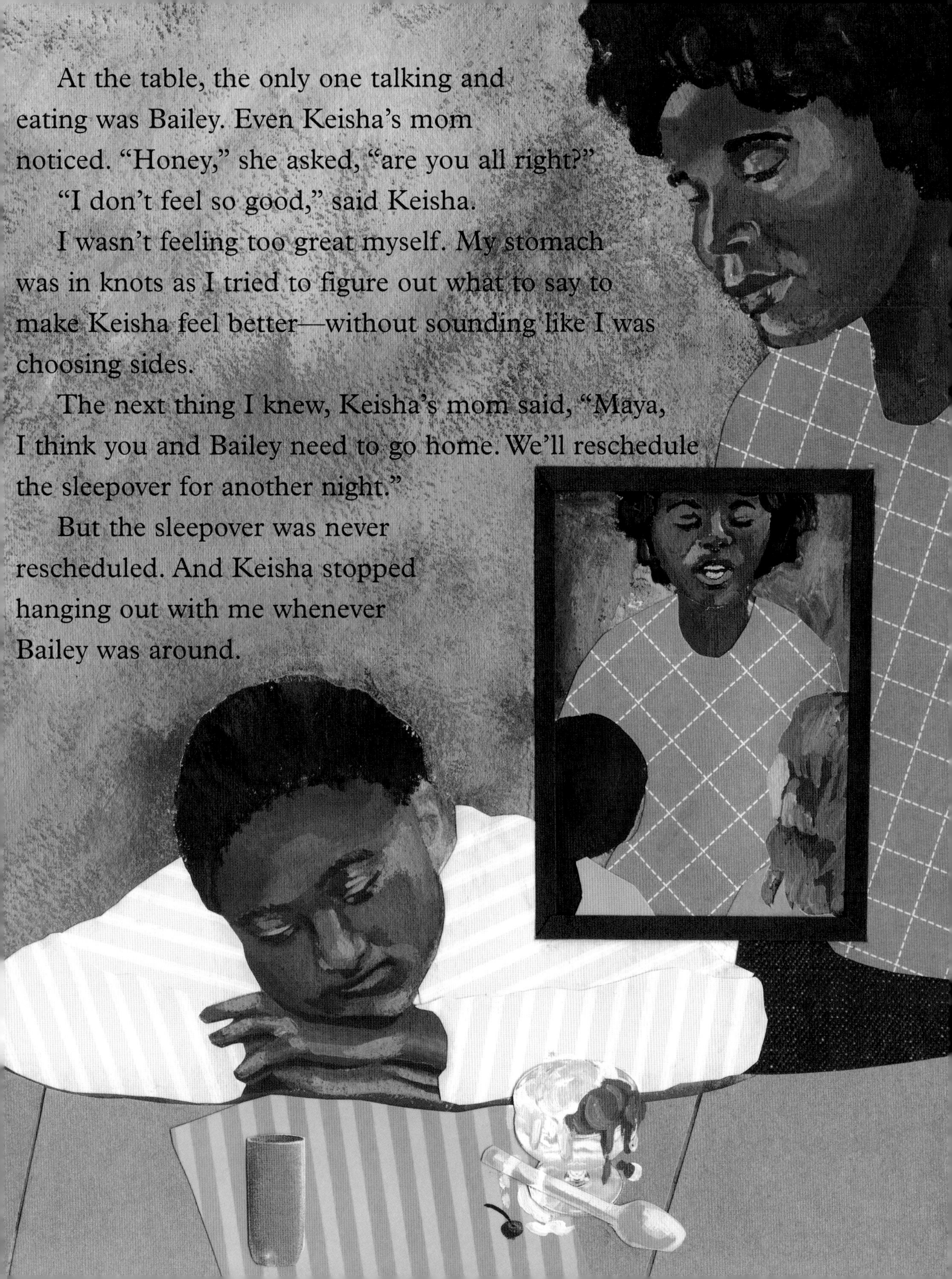

At the table, the only one talking and eating was Bailey. Even Keisha's mom noticed. "Honey," she asked, "are you all right?"

"I don't feel so good," said Keisha.

I wasn't feeling too great myself. My stomach was in knots as I tried to figure out what to say to make Keisha feel better—without sounding like I was choosing sides.

The next thing I knew, Keisha's mom said, "Maya, I think you and Bailey need to go home. We'll reschedule the sleepover for another night."

But the sleepover was never rescheduled. And Keisha stopped hanging out with me whenever Bailey was around.

Then, a few weeks ago at recess, Bailey and I were at the swings and we overheard Lizzy telling Hua that she thought Brian, the new boy in our class, was "kind of cute."

"Ooohh . . . so you like Brian?" interrupted Bailey.

"She didn't say that," snapped Hua.

"I bet he likes you too," said Bailey. "You want me to find out?"

"NO!" shrieked Hua and Lizzy.

Before any of us could stop her, Bailey ran over to Brian. I chased after her, shouting, "Don't do it!"

But Bailey didn't listen. She was all mouth and no ears.

"Oh Briii-an," said Bailey. "Guess whaaa-at? Lizzy thinks you're cute. I think she likes you. Do you like Lizzy?"

Brian's face turned bright red as the boys around him made kissy noises.

"It's okay, you can tell me. I'm good friends with Lizzy."

Before he could answer, I pulled Bailey away. "Cut it out—you're embarrassing him!"

CARLETON PLACE
PUBLIC LIBRARY

By the time we were back at the swings, my head was pounding, Lizzy was in tears, and Hua was steaming mad.

"Bailey McKenna," yelled Hua, "you've got a BIG, FAT MOUTH! Why don't you mind your own business?!"

"That wasn't very nice what you just said!" Bailey countered. "You'll be sorry!"

A few days later, there was a rumor going around school that Hua had written nasty words on the girls' bathroom wall. I knew she didn't do it. I also knew who started the rumor: Bailey.

Then things went from bad to worse. When Bailey was at my house a couple of Saturdays later, she overheard Dad and Mom arguing about money. I was embarrassed, but I didn't think it was the end of the world. Everybody's parents fight at some time or another—right?

That Monday morning, I saw Bailey whispering to some kids and pointing at me. I couldn't figure out what was going on until Keisha stopped me in the hallway.

"I'm sorry to hear about your parents," she said.

"What about them?"

"Well, you know, that they're getting a divorce . . ."

"WHAT? My parents aren't getting a divorce! Who told you that?"

"I heard it from Lizzy. Bailey told her."

I suddenly felt sick to my stomach. "But it's not true!"

Before I could say anything more, the bell rang for class.

Mrs. Rodriguez started talking about the life cycle of insects, but I wasn't listening; there was too much buzzing going on inside my own head.

I felt a light touch on my shoulder. “Maya, are you okay?” Mrs. Rodriguez asked.

“Not really.”

“Does this have to do with what’s going on at home?”

Oh, no! I bet she’d heard the rumor too!

“Why don’t you go to the counselor’s office and talk with Ms. Bloom,” she suggested.

It sounded like a good idea. Ms. Bloom always cared about what I had to say.

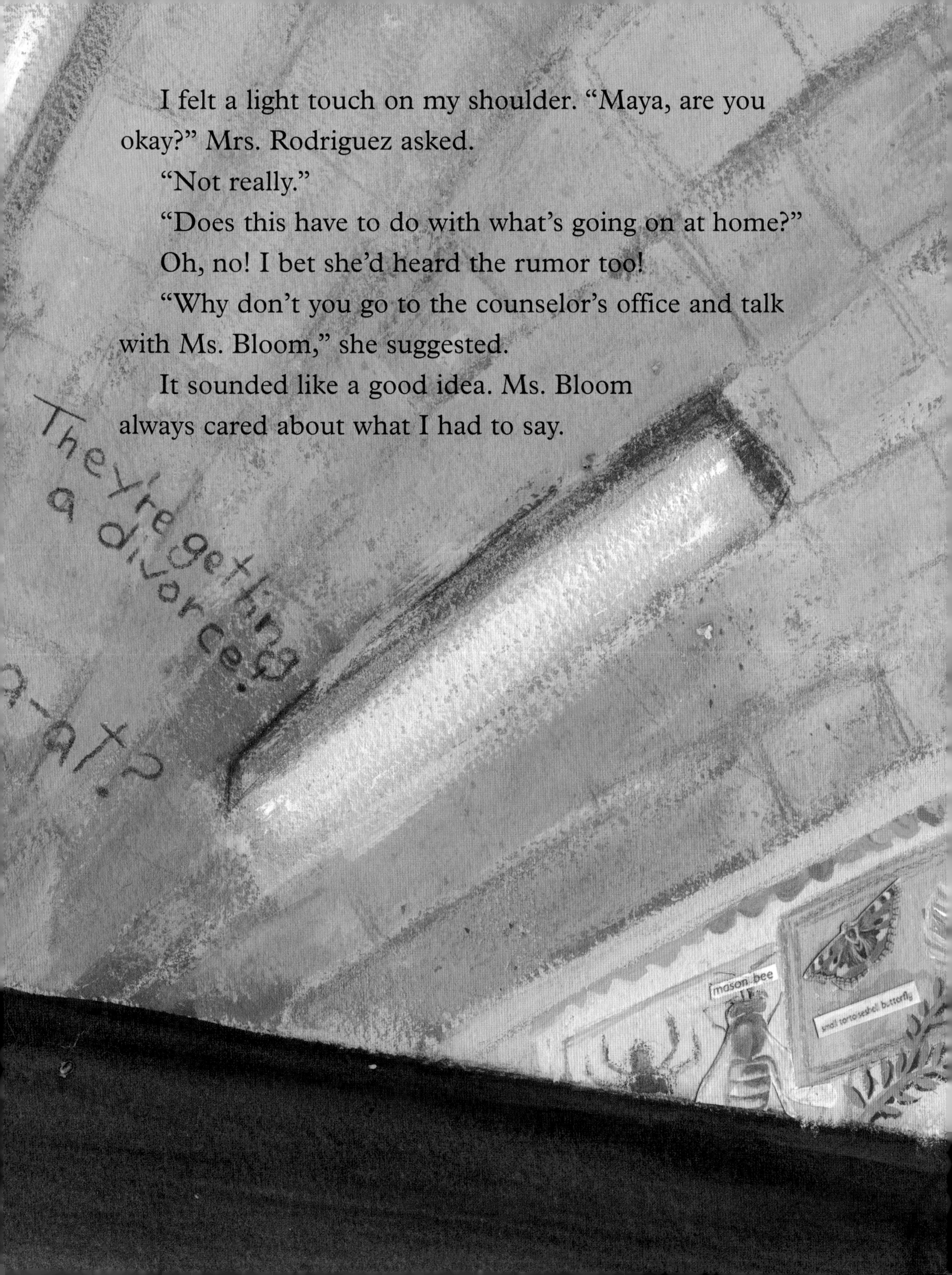

"How are you doing?"
Ms. Bloom asked.
"Not so great."

I told her how Bailey said things to my friends that were really mean or embarrassing. "I ask her to stop, but she doesn't listen. Now she's telling everyone that my parents are getting a divorce and it's NOT true!"

“Hmmm,” said Ms. Bloom. “It sounds like Bailey has a bad case of trouble talk.”

“Trouble what?”

“Trouble talk,” repeated Ms. Bloom. “Spreading rumors, saying hurtful things, and sharing information that isn’t hers to share are examples of the kind of talk that leads to nothing but trouble.”

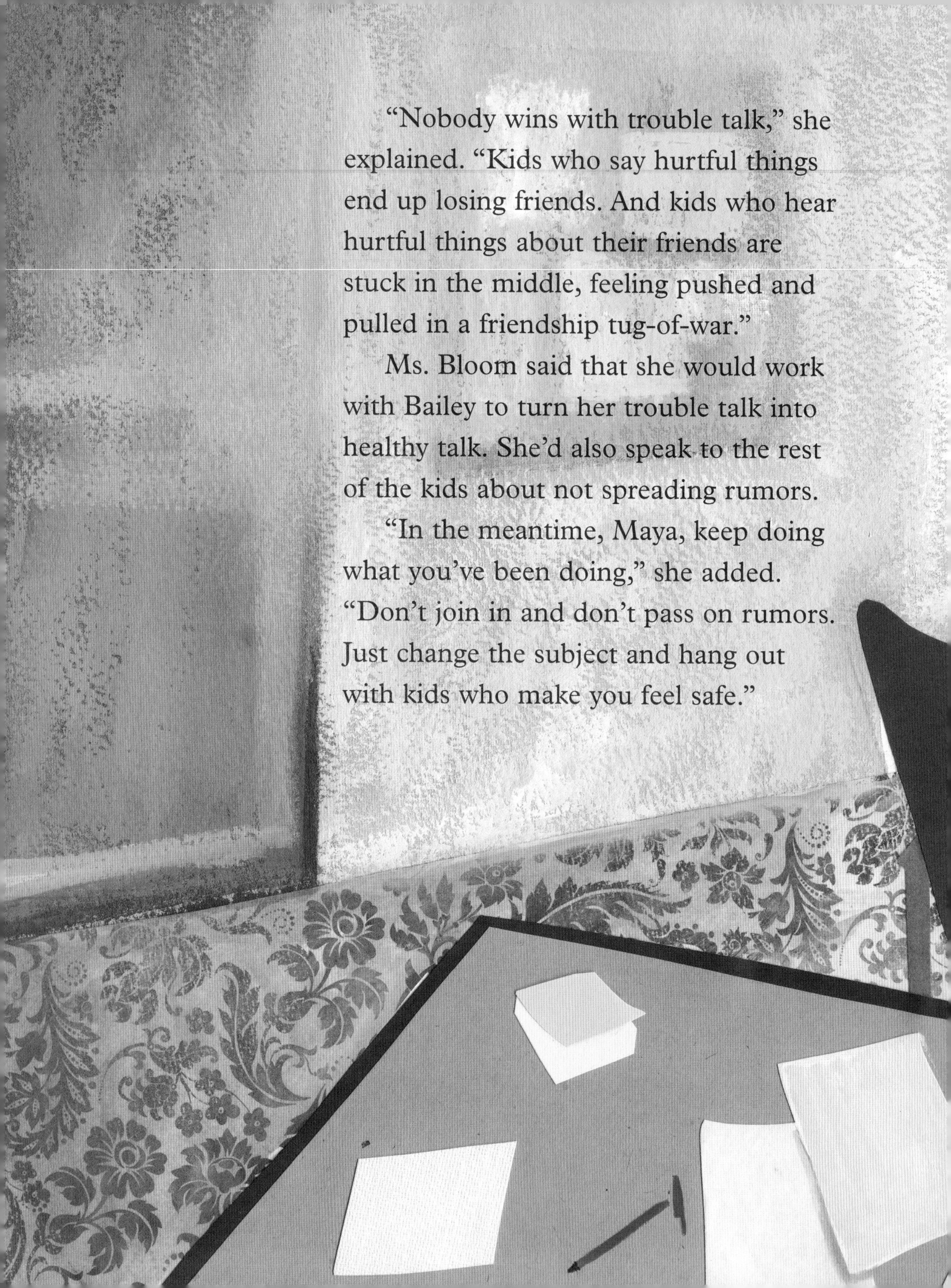

"Nobody wins with trouble talk," she explained. "Kids who say hurtful things end up losing friends. And kids who hear hurtful things about their friends are stuck in the middle, feeling pushed and pulled in a friendship tug-of-war."

Ms. Bloom said that she would work with Bailey to turn her trouble talk into healthy talk. She'd also speak to the rest of the kids about not spreading rumors.

"In the meantime, Maya, keep doing what you've been doing," she added. "Don't join in and don't pass on rumors. Just change the subject and hang out with kids who make you feel safe."

I ended up staying away from Bailey. I knew it made her sad, but it's hard to be friends with someone you don't trust. And I didn't trust Bailey.

Lately, I've noticed Bailey is trying hard to stop her trouble talk. She even wrote "I'm sorry" cards to Keisha, Lizzy, Hua, and me. It was nice to get the card. I knew it wasn't easy for her to write it.

Mom says it takes a brave person to want to change. And that it takes an open heart to accept that people can change. That got me thinking. . . . There are still a lot of things I like about Bailey. Maybe some day I'll be able to trust her again. When you have an open heart, anything's possible!

Author's Note: More about Trouble Talk

In this story, I define "trouble talk" as any kind of talk ". . . that leads to nothing but trouble." Gossiping; spreading rumors; lying; giving hurtful, unsolicited opinions or advice; and sharing information that is not yours to share are prime examples of trouble talk.

According to the latest research on relational aggression—the use of relationships to manipulate and hurt others—trouble talk is a growing problem in school, at home, and especially online. Computers, cell phones, and other communication devices are being used to quickly spread hurtful material on a wide-scale basis. Experts report that kids who are targets of gossip, rumors, humiliation, and intentional exclusion find it more harmful than physical bullying. And, as with Maya in *Trouble Talk,* bystanders who witness these acts of aggression suffer physiologically and psychologically as well. Stomachaches, headaches, stress, anxiety, and depression are common symptoms bystanders may experience.

Turning Trouble Talk into Healthy Talk

How can we encourage children to engage in healthier friendships? Below are my suggestions, along with those recommended by Drs. Charisse Nixon and Cheryl Dellasega in their book, *Girl Wars: 12 Strategies That Will End Female Bullying.*

- Catch children in the act of kindness and acknowledge it.
- Connect with your children's friends . . . and their parents.
- Help children establish healthy boundaries in their friendships.
- Find or create safe spaces for children at risk.
- Promote positive emotional expression through journaling and role-playing.
- Extend children's support network of people who care about them.
- Be a good listener and friendship role model yourself—don't be a Trouble Talker.
- Role-play with children to improve their critical-thinking skills and problem-solving strategies.
- Balance computer and phone time with face-to-face encounters.
- If it's beyond your ability to help, talk to a professional.

Empowering Bystanders

How do we empower bystanders like Maya in this story to stand up to trouble talk without subjecting them to the very real risk of retaliation by the trouble talker/aggressor? Stan Davis, anti-bullying consultant and founder of www.stopbullyingnow.com, has found that a non-confrontational approach (e.g., silence, a shrug, or a gentle change of subject), combined with a determination not to spread the rumor to anyone else, works best to minimize risk of counter-aggression. And because rumors don't spread unless more than one person spreads them, educating children of all ages on their pivotal role as bystanders who can make or break a rumor is critical in squelching trouble talk.

For more information, please refer to Additional Resources.

Trudy Ludwig

QUESTIONS FOR DISCUSSION

"No offense, but . . . ."

Do the words "no offense" make what Bailey said to Keisha less insulting? Why or why not?

Have you ever had someone say "no offense" to you before saying something negative about you? How did that make you feel?

Was Bailey really doing Keisha a favor by telling her the truth in *Truth or Dare*? Why or why not?

"It's okay, you can tell me. I'm good friends with Lizzy."

Was it okay for Bailey to tell Brian that Lizzy liked him when Lizzy told her not to?

Has anyone ever shared your secrets with other kids? If yes, how did that make you feel?

Which takes longer—building trust or destroying it? Explain.

"That wasn't nice what you just said. You'll be sorry!"

What does it mean when someone says, "You'll be sorry"?

Bailey spreads a rumor about Hua because Hua said that Bailey had "a big, fat mouth." Why do you think Bailey spread a rumor about Maya's parents getting a divorce?

Maya suspected her teacher, Mrs. Rodriguez, heard the divorce rumor and thought it might be true. Do you think grownups are capable of believing and/or spreading rumors just like kids? Explain.

Why do people spread rumors? What do they get out of it?

". . . kids who hear hurtful things about their friends . . . [feel] pushed and pulled in a friendship tug-of-war."

Were you ever the kid in the middle, watching one friend hurt another friend? If yes, how did it make you feel? Did you do anything about it?

What did Ms. Bloom suggest bystanders do to help targets of trouble talk, without risking their own safety? Do you have other suggestions?

Dr. Martin Luther King, Jr. said, "In the end, we will remember not the words of our enemies, but the silence of our friends." What does this quote mean to you?

When you have an open heart, anything's possible!

Do you believe people are capable of changing for the better?

Do you think Bailey deserves a second chance if she is truly making an effort to change?

What would it take for Bailey to regain Maya's trust and friendship?

Additional Resources

ORGANIZATIONS

Girls Inc.®
120 Wall Street
New York, NY 10005-3902
www.girlsinc.org

Hands & Words Are Not For Hurting Project®
PO Box 2644
Salem, OR 97308-2644
www.handsproject.org

International Bullying Prevention Association (IBPA)
PO Box 2288
East Falmouth, MA 02536
www.stopbullyingworld.com

Operation Respect
2 Penn Plaza, 5th Floor
New York, NY 10121
www.operationrespect.org

The Ophelia Project®
718 Nevada Drive
Erie, PA 16505
www.opheliaproject.org

WEBSITES

www.bullying.org
www.cyberbully.org
www.girlsleadershipinstitute.org
www.stopbullyingnow.com
www.stopbullyingnow.hrsa.gov/index.asp

RECOMMENDED READINGS

For Adults:

Borba, Michele, Ed.D. *Nobody Likes Me, Everybody Hates Me: The Top 25 Friendship Problems and How to Solve Them.* San Francisco: Jossey-Bass, 2005.

Davis, Stan. *Schools Where Everyone Belongs: Practical Strategies for Reducing Bullying.* Champaign: Research Press, 2005.

Dellasega, Cheryl, Ph.D., and Charisse Nixon, Ph.D. *Girl Wars: 12 Strategies That Will End Female Bullying.* New York: Simon & Schuster, 2003.

Simmons, Rachel. *Odd Girl Out: The Hidden Culture of Aggression in Girls.* New York: Harcourt, 2002.

Thompson, Michael, Lawrence J. Cohen, and Catherine O'Neill Grace. *Best Friends, Worst Enemies: Understanding the Social Lives of Children.* New York: Ballantine Books, 2001.

Wiseman, Rosalind. *Queen Bees and Wannabees: Helping Your Daughter Survive Cliques, Gossip, Boyfriends and Other Realities of Adolescence.* New York: Crown Publishers, 2002.

For Children:

Brown, Laurie Krasney and Marc Brown. *How To Be A Friend: A Guide to Making Friends and Keeping Them.* New York: Little Brown & Co., 2001.

Carlson, Nancy. *How To Lose All Your Friends Fast.* New York: Puffin, 1997.

Criswell, Patti Kelley. *A Smart Girl's Guide to Friendship Troubles.* Middleton: American Girl, LLC, 2003.

Estes, Eleanor. *The Hundred Dresses.* New York: Scholastic, 1973.

Ludwig, Trudy. *My Secret Bully.* Berkeley: Tricycle Press, 2005.

Ludwig, Trudy. *Just Kidding.* Berkeley: Tricycle Press, 2006.

Ludwig, Trudy. *Sorry!* Berkeley: Tricycle Press, 2006.

Madonna. *Mr. Peabody's Apples.* New York: Callaway, 2003.

Moss, Peggy. *Our Friendship Rules.* Gardiner: Tilbury House, 2007.

Romain, Trevor. *Cliques, Phonies, & Other Baloney.* Minneapolis: Free Spirit Publishing, 1998.

For Trouble Talkers everywhere—have the courage to change.–T.L.

To my husband, Cameron.–M.P.

This is a work of fiction. All names, characters, places, and incidents are either the author's imagination or used fictitiously. No reference to any real person is intended or should be inferred. Likeness of any situations to any persons living or dead is purely coincidental.

Text copyright © 2008 by Trudy Ludwig
Illustrations copyright © 2008 by Mikela Prevost

All rights reserved. No part of this book may be reproduced in any form without the written permission of the publisher, except in the case of brief quotations embodied in critical articles or reviews.

Tricycle Press
an imprint of Ten Speed Press
PO Box 7123
Berkeley, California 94707
www.tricyclepress.com

Design by Tasha Hall
Typeset in Plantin and Whoa Nelly
The illustrations in this book were rendered in watercolor, gouache, acrylic, and collage.

Library of Congress Cataloging-in-Publication Data
Ludwig, Trudy.
Trouble Talk / by Trudy Ludwig; illustrated by Mikela Prevost; foreword by Charisse L. Nixon, Ph.D.
p. cm.
Summary: Maya gets help from a school counselor when the new student she has tried to befriend upsets her, as she has other students, by spreading rumors, saying hurtful things, and sharing information that is not hers to share.
ISBN 978-1-58246-240-0
[1. Gossip—Fiction. 2. Behavior—Fiction. 3. Interpersonal relations—Fiction. 4. Schools—Fiction.] I. Prevost, Mikela, ill. II. Title.
PZ7.L98865Big 2007
[E]—dc22

2007019022

First Tricycle Press printing, 2008
Printed in China
1 2 3 4 5 6 – 12 11 10 09 08

CARLETON PLACE
PUBLIC LIBRARY